YASMIN

written by
SAADIA FARUQI

illustrated by
HATEM ALY

PICTURE WINDOW BOOKS
a capstone imprint

To Mariam for inspiring me, and Mubashir
for helping me find the right words—S.F.

To my sister, Eman, and her amazing girls,
Jana and Kenzi—H.A.

Yasmin is published by Picture Window Books, an imprint of Capstone.
1710 Roe Crest Drive
North Mankato, Minnesota 56003
www.capstonepub.com

Text copyright © 2020 by Saadia Faruqi.
Illustrations copyright © 2020 by Capstone.

Library of Congress Cataloging-in-Publication Data is available on
the Library of Congress website.
ISBN: 978-1-5158-4642-0 (hardcover)
ISBN: 978-1-5158-5886-7 (paperback)
ISBN: 978-1-5158-4647-5 (eBook PDF)

Summary: Everyone in Yasmin's gym class is excited to play soccer,
except for Yasmin. She's seen the pros play, and it looks scary! When
Yasmin is chosen as goalie, will she step up or back out?

Editorial Credits:
Kristen Mohn, editor; Lori Bye and Kay Fraser, designers; Jo Miller,
media researcher; Tori Abraham, production specialist

Design Elements:
Shutterstock: Art and Fashion, rangsan paidaen

TABLE OF CONTENTS

CHAPTER 1

A New Coach

...... for gym class.
Principal Nguyen had some news.

"Students, we have a new gym teacher," he said. "Please welcome Coach Garcia to our school!"

"Welcome, Coach Garcia!" the students all said together.

Yasmin looked at the new coach. She looked very important with her ~~~ ~ ~ ~ ~

"Four square? Freeze tag?"

Coach Garcia shook her head. "Soccer!" she announced. She lifted a soccer ball over her head.

Ali cheered. "Hooray! I love soccer!"

Yasmin frowned. She'd watched lots of soccer on TV with Baba. The players kicked and elbowed and fell down a lot. It looked dangerous.

"I've never played soccer before," she said quietly.

Coach Garcia heard her. "I'm here to teach you," she replied. "It's good to try new things."

Yasmin groaned.

CHAPTER 2

Excuses

Coach Garcia explained the rules of the game. Then she showed the students some moves.

She stopped the ball with her feet. "This is called trapping," she said.

She kicked the ball while
running. "And this is dribbling!"

"Now it's your turn," Coach
Garcia said.

Ali already knew how to play.

He kicked the ball as hard as he

could into the net.

Yasmin wondered if it hurt his

feet to kick like that.

Emma bounced the ball off

her knee. That looked like it

really hurt.

Yasmin stayed near
Coach Garcia. "Can I be the
cheerleader?" she asked. "I can
yell really loudly."

Coach Garcia shook her head.
"Everyone has to play."

Yasmin watched the others
kick and dribble and trap. One
boy tripped and fell.

"Can I be the water girl?" she

Coach Garcia blew her whistle loudly and clapped. "Ready for a game?"

She put the students into teams.

"Can I be the referee? I remember all the rules you taught us," Yasmin begged.

Coach Garcia pointed to the net. "You get to be the goalie," she said firmly.

"*Goalie?*" Yasmin asked with a gulp.

She remembered how Ali
had kicked the ball into the
net. Goalie looked like the most
dangerous job of all.

CHAPTER 3

The Goalkeeper

Yasmin stood inside the goal. She wanted to hide.

Ali kicked the ball. Yasmin ducked. The ball went right into the net. Ali's team cheered.

"Goalies can use their hands," Coach Garcia reminded Yasmin.

Soon Ali's team kicked the

ball toward the goal again. This

time Yasmin jumped to catch it.

She missed.

"Goal!" shouted Ali.

Coach Garcia called out,

"Good try, Yasmin!"

Yasmin got ready again.

Soon Ali's ball came right at her feet. She rushed toward it—and tripped. But she stopped the ball!

"You did it, Yasmin!" Emma cheered. "You blocked the goal!"

Yasmin got up slowly. "I did?"

Coach Garcia gave her a high five. "Great job, goalie!"

"You're the star of the team, Yasmin!" Emma said. "Can you teach me that move you did?"

"You were just like the pros on TV!" Ali said.

Yasmin grinned and wiped

the sweat off her face.

"It wasn't even that

dangerous," she told them.

Coach Garcia offered her a

bottle of water. "*I'll* be the water

water.

"Thanks, Coach," she said.

"Who's ready to play again?"

Think About It, Talk About It

* Yasmin is worried about trying something that is new and scary to her. Think of a time you tried something new. How did you give yourself courage?

* If you were on Yasmin's soccer team, what name would you give your team? Why?

* Yasmin watches soccer with her father. Is there a sport or activity that your parents have shared with you? What activity would you like to do with your parents if you could pick anything?

baba (BAH-bah)—father

hijab (HEE-jahb)—scarf covering the hair

jaan (jahn)—life; a sweet nickname for a loved one

kameez (kuh-MEEZ)—long tunic or shirt

lassi (LAH-see)—yogurt drink

mama (MAH-mah)—mother

nana (NAH-nah)—grandfather on mother's side

nani (NAH-nee)—grandmother on mother's side

salaam (sah-LAHM)—hello

shukriya (shuh-KREE-yuh)—thank you

Pakistani Fun Facts

Yasmin and her family are proud of their Pakistani culture. Yasmin loves to share facts about Pakistan!

Location

Pakistan is on the continent of Asia, with India on one side and Afghanistan on the other.

Islamabad

PAKISTAN

Population

Pakistan's population is more than 200,000,000 people. It is the world's sixth-most-populous country.

Sports

The most popular sport in Pakistan is a bat-and-ball game called cricket. Soccer is also very popular there, but it's called football.

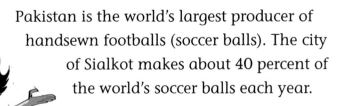

Pakistan is the world's largest producer of handsewn footballs (soccer balls). The city of Sialkot makes about 40 percent of the world's soccer balls each year.

Design Your Own Soccer Jersey!

- scissors
- tape

STEPS:

1. Lay the paper over this page and trace the front of the jersey.

2. Use markers or colored pencils to create a design on the traced jersey. What colors and designs will your team have? What will your team name be?

3. Cut out your jersey and tape it to your mirror or a notebook to show your team spirit!

About the Author

Saadia Faruqi is a Pakistani American writer, interfaith activist, and cultural sensitivity trainer previously profiled in *O Magazine*. She is editor-in-chief of *Blue Minaret*, a magazine for Muslim art, poetry, and prose. Saadia is also author of the adult short story collection, *Brick Walls: Tales of Hope & Courage from Pakistan*. Her essays have been published in *Huffington Post*, *Upworthy*, and *NBC Asian America*. She resides in Houston, Texas, with her husband and children.

Hatem Aly is an Egyptian-born illustrator whose work has been featured in multiple publications worldwide. He currently lives in beautiful New Brunswick, Canada, with his wife, son, and more pets than people. When he is not dipping cookies in a cup of tea or staring at blank pieces of paper, he is usually drawing books. One of the books he illustrated is *The Inquisitor's Tale* by Adam Gidwitz, which won a Newbery Honor and other awards, despite Hatem's drawings of a farting dragon, a two-headed cat, and stinky cheese.

Join Yasmin
on all her adventures!

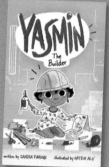